Letter to the Lake

Susan Marie Swanson
Peter Catalanotto

JANUARY

Rosie's Room

A Richard Jackson Book

DK Publishing, Inc.

Dear Lake,
    When I think of you, I think of rocks hiding under the waves, like secrets. Remember me, your friend Rosie? Remember me?

Everything has been snow and ice for a long time. It is morning now, but still dark. The radio voices keep talking about troubles and cold. Mama is going to take me to school on the way to her job. I can tell she's got a lot on her mind because her sweater is buttoned crooked. Our windows rattle, trying to get warm.

Lake, I think of you all winter long. I know you are still there. Why do you have to be so far away? What do you think about in winter, when waves turn to ice?

Remember last summer, how I went out before breakfast to pick raspberries? Remember how I pretended a piece of bark was my breakfast bowl?

I'm having toast for breakfast, with lots of raspberry jam. The kitchen window is covered over with frost. I keep some rocks from last summer on the windowsill. They feel cold when I pick them up.

One of the rocks looks like a bear's paw. Remember when I found the place where the bear left tracks in the mud?

One rock is as smooth as a candle. The speckles on it remind me of dragonflies darting after bugs.

My best rock is shaped like a house, like the little house where we stay when we visit you. I'm going to carry that house in my pocket today.

Mama and I have to go outside and shovel our car out of the snow again. My boots are getting too small. I keep losing mittens, so now I don't have two that match.

It is hard work to scrape the snow and ice off the car windows so that we can see out. The cranky car engine won't start. Mama sighs. She puts her hands over her face. But when I say we should go get our friend Becky to help us, she looks at me and smiles.

Mama helps me tighten my scarf, and we walk through the freezing wind, up the block toward Becky's house.

I keep thinking about you, Lake, every step of the way. Remember me? Remember me floating in a silver boat, pulling hard on the oars? I want to row all the way to summer, where you float the water lilies, and the loons, and the whole bright sky.

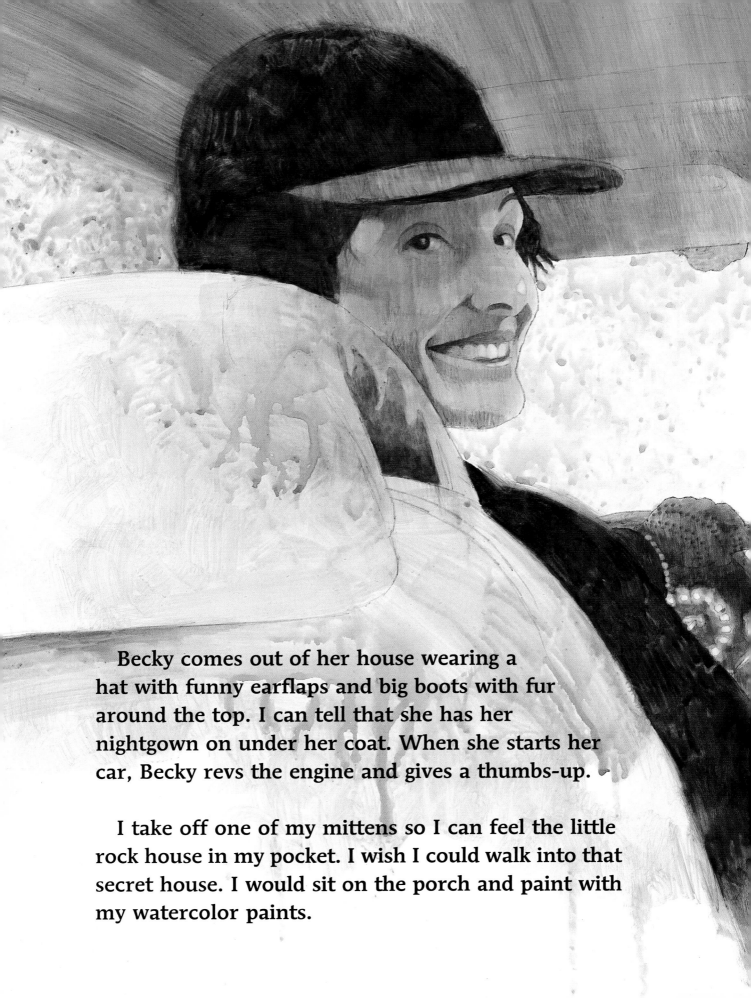

Becky comes out of her house wearing a
hat with funny earflaps and big boots with fur
around the top. I can tell that she has her
nightgown on under her coat. When she starts her
car, Becky revs the engine and gives a thumbs-up.

I take off one of my mittens so I can feel the little
rock house in my pocket. I wish I could walk into that
secret house. I would sit on the porch and paint with
my watercolor paints.

Oh, I'd paint the green trees leaning over you, then a heron that just landed on an old log.

I'd paint the dragonflies and our silver rowboat. To paint you, Lake, I'd make as many colors of blue as I could. Remember me, floating with the sky?

Becky drives her car up to ours.

She pulls out the jumper cables, and Mama opens up the hoods of the cars. We all stamp and hug ourselves to keep from shivering. The jumper cables hook our cold engine up to Becky's. Mama turns the key and turns it again.

Our car grumbles and shudders before it starts.
Becky throws the jumper cables over her shoulder,
slams the hood, and waves good-bye. The car wheels
spin and skid all the gray-and-white way to my school.
Mama is singing bits and pieces of a song.

She says it is an old song from Norway, about melting snow, but she doesn't know the whole song. Sometimes she hums where there are supposed to be words.

The sun is lighting up the gray clouds. Right when I am looking, the streetlights snap off!

The rock in my pocket feels warm now. You know what, Lake? I think it's Mama's turn to have this rock.

When we get back
to summer, I will throw
rock after rock, and you'll
draw circles in the spot where
each one falls. *Plop,* the rocks
will say. *Gulp. Hiccup. Hop.*
You'll hide those rocks under
the waves, and I'll put some more
in my pockets, to keep like secrets
the whole winter long.
Remember? Remember me?

Your friend,

Rosie

For Benjamin and Nicholas
—S.M.S.

For Ms. Nuss, Ms. Gallagher, Ms. Gerhart, and Ms. Sinn
—P.C.

Special thanks to Paula and Aimee Woods
—P.C.

A Richard Jackson Book

DK Publishing, Inc.
95 Madison Avenue
New York, New York 10016
Visit us on the World Wide Web at http://www.dk.com
Text copyright © 1998 by Susan Marie Swanson.
Illustrations copyright © 1998 by Peter Catalanotto.

Library of Congress Cataloging-in-Publication Data
Swanson, Susan Marie.
  Letter to the Lake / by Susan Marie Swanson ; illustrated by Peter
Catalanotto. — 1st ed.
    p. cm.
  Summary: On a cold winter day, Rosie writes a letter to the lake
where she loves to spend time during the summer.
  ISBN 0-7894-2483-5
  [1. Lakes—Fiction. 2. Winter—Fiction. 3. Summer—Fiction.
4. Letters—Fiction.] I. Catalanotto, Peter, ill. II. Title.
PZ7.S97255Le 1997[E]—dc21 97-34107 CIP AC

The text of this book is set in 16 point ITC Mendoza Medium.
Printed and bound in USA.
First Edition, 1998
10 9 8 7 6 5 4 3 2 1